Heart beating fast, Sienna pushed the button. What would happen? From deep inside the earth a rumbling started and the ground began to gently shake. Stone grated against stone and then slowly but surely the whole of the grassy mound sank into the ground, taking them all with it!

HAVE YOU READ?

Sophia and Rainbow

Scarlett and Blaze

Ava and Star

Isabel and Cloud

Layla and Dancer

Olivia and Snowflake

Rosa and Crystal

Ariana and Whisper

Matilda and Pearl

Freya and Honey

Violet and Twinkle

Isla and Buttercup

Lily and Feather

Phoebe and Shimmer

Zara and Moonbeam

Aisha and Silver

Lyra and Misty

Evie and Sunshine

Ivy and Flame

UNICORN ACADEMY
...Where magic happens!

Sienna and Sparkle

JULIE SYKES

illustrated by
LUCY TRUMAN

nosy crow

To Lucy Truman, for her wonderful illustration magic.

First published in the UK in 2022 by Nosy Crow Ltd
The Crow's Nest, 14 Baden Place
Crosby Row, London, SE1 1YW

Nosy Crow Eireann Ltd
44 Orchard Grove, Kenmare, Co Kerry, V93 FY22, Ireland

www.nosycrow.com

ISBN: 978 1 78800 986 7

A CIP catalogue record for this book is available from the British Library.

Printed and bound in Great Britain by Clays Ltd, Elcograf S.p.A.

Papers used by Nosy Crow are made from
wood grown in sustainable forests.

MIX
Paper from
responsible sources
FSC
www.fsc.org   FSC® C018072

1 3 5 7 9 10 8 6 4 2

CHAPTER ONE

"Over here, Lyra!" Sienna called as Lyra galloped past on her unicorn Misty.

It was a chilly winter's day and Sienna and her friends from Ruby dorm were playing a crossnet match with the Topaz dorm boys. The score was six-all and the match was almost over.

Sienna and her unicorn, Sparkle, were in easy reach of the goal. She waved her racket impatiently. "Lyra, to me! I can win this for us!"

Lyra threw the ball and Sienna deftly caught it.

"Go!" she urged Sparkle, who raced for the goal – a net suspended in a tree. *We're going to win,*

Sienna thought excitedly.

Evie whooped as her unicorn, Sunshine, galloped enthusiastically alongside Sparkle.

"Out of my way, Evie!" Sienna exclaimed as she launched the ball at the goal.

Sunshine swerved away, surprising Evie who yelled and waved her stick in the air as she recovered her balance. The ball clipped the top of her stick and dropped into her net.

Evie stared at the ball in astonishment. "I caught it!"

"Yes, but it was supposed to go into the *goal*!" Sienna shouted in frustration. "Pass it back so I can shoot again!"

Evie tried to throw the ball back, but it flew off at an angle, arching high over the goal and bouncing outside the pitch. "Whoops!" she said.

"Evie!" wailed Sienna.

Jumping down from Sparkle, Sienna ran to the pile of leaves she thought it had fallen into. She rummaged around, throwing leaves into the air. Where was it? There were only a few minutes of match time left to win the game.

Sam galloped over to join her and began raking the leaves with his racket. "Finders keepers," he said, grinning. "Come and help, guys," he called over his shoulder to his dorm-mates. Let's find the ball and score the winning goal!"

Sienna scowled. There was no way she was letting the boys find the ball first! "Sparkle!" she shouted, looking around and seeing her unicorn chatting with his friends. "What are you doing over there? I need your help!"

"Sorry," Sparkle called cheerfully. "Coming, Sienna." He trotted over and started pushing through the leaves with his nose. "Nope, not here… Or here." He looked up, leaves decorating his face.

"I vote we give up," said Ivy, riding over with the others. "It's cold and I'm hungry."

Evie nodded. "It must be nearly dinner time."

"Yeah, it's been fun," said Lyra. "But let's call it a draw and go in."

"No way!" protested Sienna.

"Sienna's right – we're not giving up yet," said Reuben, who was searching with the other boys.

Storm, Reuben's unicorn, stamped his hoof.

"I'll help find it," he said eagerly.

A familiar sugary smell drifted past Sienna. *That smells like magic*, she realised. Suddenly a sparkling blue arrow appeared above Storm. "What's happening?!" Reuben exclaimed.

They all gaped at the quivering arrow. It hovered above Storm for a moment and then shot away to a nearby bush where it pointed downwards, bobbing up and down.

Storm whinnied in delight. "Reuben, I must have finding magic just like my great-uncle!"

"That's amazing!" said Reuben, hugging him. "Finding magic sounds awesome. How does it work?"

If we follow the arrow, I think we'll find the ball." Storm trotted to the bush.

Reuben ran after him and, falling on to his tummy, wriggled underneath. A few seconds later he reappeared, holding up the ball. "Storm did it! He's the best!"

Forgetting about the match, everyone crowded round to congratulate them.

"You've both bonded too," Lyra said, pointing at a green and silver streak that had appeared in Reuben's dark fringe.

Bonding was the highest form of friendship between a student and their unicorn. When it happened, a lock of the student's hair turned the same colour as their unicorn's mane. Students and their unicorns came to Unicorn Academy to train to be guardians of the beautiful island where they lived. During their time at the academy the students had to find their unicorn's magic and

bond. If that hadn't happened by the end of the first year, they returned for a second year.

"This means everyone in Topaz is going to be able to graduate together at the end of term!" exclaimed Sam.

The boys cheered and high-fived each other. Lyra, Evie and Ivy joined in, but Sienna felt her stomach twist into a knot. She and Sparkle were the only pair in Ruby dorm not to have found their magic or bonded, and she was finding it harder and harder to deal with. The school year ended in a week and she couldn't bear it if all her friends graduated and she didn't.

"Right," called Sam, "since we're now out of match time, I'm officially declaring this game a draw."

As the others started collecting the sticks and balls, Sienna rode away on Sparkle. She felt too cross and upset to join in with the post-match

chatting and joking.

"Is everything all right, Sienna?" Sparkle asked her.

"Not really," she muttered. "Oh, Sparkle. Why haven't you found your magic yet?" She patted his multicoloured mane. "Are you sure you haven't noticed anything? Any mysterious coloured sparks or anything unusual at all?"

"I don't think so," said Sparkle. "Sorry."

Sienna felt a rush of frustration. She loved Sparkle. He was very easy-going and naturally happy – but that was the problem! *He doesn't try hard enough*, she thought.

"I wonder what my powers will be when I do get them?" said Sparkle. "Having finding magic like Storm's would be fun but I'd rather have something really cool like flying magic or fire magic or maybe exploding magic like Sunshine. BAM!" He jumped into a drift of leaves, sending

them flying. "POW!"

Sienna couldn't help but giggle. Sparkle's laid-back nature might annoy her at times but he always cheered her up when she was feeling grumpy. "You doughnut! You're crazy!"

"But you love me?" Sparkle said hopefully.

"Yes," she said, leaning down and hugging him. "Of course I do!"

When they reached the stable block, Sienna pulled off her gloves and dismounted. It was cosy and warm inside and the air was filled with the sweet smell of sky berries – the unicorns' favourite

food. She dodged round one of the automatic trollies that trundled up and down the aisles and followed Sparkle into his stall to brush him down.

Sparkle had a snow-white coat patterned with rainbows and a multicoloured mane and tail. Sienna thought he was the prettiest out of all the unicorns. If only he had his magic, he would be perfect!

She topped up his water and hay, adding an extra-large helping of sky berries to his feed bucket. *Sky berries strengthen unicorns' magic so maybe an extra portion will help Sparkle to find his power*, she thought hopefully.

She didn't feel like listening to the others discussing Storm's magic and how great it was that the boys could all graduate together, so as soon as Sparkle was settled she said goodnight to him and set off across the school grounds for

her dorm. The first stars were just starting to twinkle and Unicorn Academy rose up in front of her, its marble and glass turrets and towers silhouetted against the darkening sky.

I love it here, but I don't want to stay another year without all my friends. Oh, I hope Sparkle finds his magic soon!

CHAPTER TWO

"Are you OK?" Evie asked Sienna when she, Ivy and Lyra finally arrived back at the dorm.

"Yeah, how come you didn't help us clear up after the match?" said Lyra.

Sienna pulled a face. "Sorry." She'd been feeling so fed up that she'd forgotten about helping. "I … um … I wasn't feeling very well." She didn't like lying to her friends but she didn't want to explain and have them all feeling sorry for her.

"Are you feeling better now?" Ivy asked in concern.

Sienna nodded. "Yes, thanks." Jumping up, she went to the bathroom to avoid talking further.

When they had cleaned themselves up, they went down to the dining hall for dinner: cheesy pasta with garlic bread and grilled tomatoes followed by chocolate pudding. Afterwards they curled up in their dorm's cosy lounge. There were squishy red sofas and beanbags, shelves full of games to play and a fluffy red rug in front of the crackling fire.

Lyra produced a pack of cards and they played several noisy rounds of Ace the Unicorn, before abandoning the game in favour of toasting marshmallows over the fire and talking about the treasure map.

At the start of the year the girls had discovered part of an old treasure map. They'd had some exciting adventures tracking down the missing pieces, which had all been hidden in the school

grounds. Now they had the whole map, they had one last clue to decipher and then hopefully they would find the hidden treasure: the legendary Unicorn's Diamond. It had been formed from the happy tears of Daybreak, the first unicorn, on the birth of her foal, and it had the power to give anyone who held it their heart's desire. Because it was so powerful, one of the previous headteachers at the academy, Ms Evergreen, had hidden it away and no one had seen it for a hundred years.

"We've only got a week to solve the final clue," said Lyra. She took out the four pieces of the map and laid them on the floor, smoothing out the old yellowing paper. Each piece had a tiny drawing of Daybreak in one corner as well as other pictures round the edges. When the pieces were put together it was possible to make out a maze in the centre of the map with an X marking the diamond's hiding place.

"We've got to find the diamond before the end of term," said Sienna.

"Unless Dr Briar has found it already," said Ivy.

"She hasn't," said Lyra confidently. "I spoke to Sam before the match and he's sure she would tell him if she had found it — she'd want to boast about it — but he hasn't heard a word."

Sam's aunt was a famous archaeologist called Dr Angelica Briar. She had found out about the map and wanted the diamond for her private collection.

She was so determined to have it that she had put the girls in danger several times. Sam had been helping her until he had realised how ruthless she was. Now he was firmly on the girls' side.

"We really need to solve the final riddle," said Lyra.

It was written on the fourth piece of the map, the one they had most recently found. Evie read it out.

"At the point where the landmarks make a mark
The Unicorn's Diamond hides in the dark.
A maze of danger where friends must be true,
Reach the prize and you'll know what to do."

"It sounds like the diamond is hidden in a dangerous maze," said Sienna.

"Though mazes aren't usually dark," Evie pointed out. "And the first line about landmarks – what does that mean?"

Ivy groaned. "We need more clues."

"What about this?" Sienna pointed to a few faint words written on the first piece of the map they had found. "*The Northernmost Door… The Phoenix's Claw… The Salamander's Stare… The Dragon's Lair.*"

"I wonder what they mean," said Lyra. "Are they things or places?"

Sienna frowned thoughtfully. "If they're places, then they'll be marked on the magic map, won't they?"

Lyra gasped. "You're right!"

The magic map was kept in the school hall and was a model of Unicorn Island that showed everything, right down to tiny houses and trees. If you touched the place you wanted to go, the map would transport you there. Students were only allowed to use it with a teacher's permission, but Ruby dorm had broken that rule before!

"Let's sneak into the hall after lights out," Lyra said, her eyes shining. "We can look for places

with those names, and if we find them we can ask the map to take us there!"

"Ooh, yes!" said Ivy.

Sienna felt anticipation spiral through her as they all exchanged excited looks. They were going to have another night-time adventure!

They waited until lights out and then crept downstairs. They had almost reached the hall when they turned a corner and saw Ms Nettles, the academy's strict headteacher, ahead of them.

"In here, quick!" Sienna hissed, diving behind a long curtain covering a window, and everyone squeezed in with her.

Ms Nettles started walking towards them.

As her footsteps came nearer, Sienna could barely contain her giggles. Lyra put a finger to her lips warning her to be quiet. At last the headteacher passed and the corridor was silent again.

Lyra drew the curtain back. "That was close!"

"But fun!" said Sienna with a grin.

They hurried into the hall. Moonlight shone in through the domed glass roof, illuminating the magic map in the centre. The magical force field surrounding it hummed softly.

Sienna approached the map but then her steps slowed as the hum increased to an angry buzz. Sienna seemed to bump into something. "There's an obstacle in the way," she said, feeling with her hand. "It's like an invisible wall."

"The map mustn't want us to get close," said Evie.

"But why?" said Sienna in disappointment. "It's let us before."

Lyra took charge. "I'm not sure why but even if we can't use it to go anywhere tonight, we can still look at it and see if we can find places with those weird names. Can anyone see a place called the Dragon's Lair, the Salamander's Stare or the

Phoenix's Claw?"

They edged as close as the invisible force field would let them and scanned the map.

"Nope," said Ivy at last. "Nothing."

"They're not on the map," said Sienna, disappointed.

"Wait!" said Evie suddenly. "Look – in the south there is a lake with swans on and in the east there's a stone circle. Both those things are on our treasure map!"

Lyra pulled the map pieces out of her pocket and spread them on the ground. "You're right. This quarter of the treasure map has a picture of a lake with swans on in the south, just like on the magic map, and this quarter has a stone circle in the east."

"Ooh, and here," said Ivy, pointing, "is an obelisk, and I saw one in the same place on the magic map."

"The fourth drawing is of the academy, which is in the north on both maps," said Lyra.

"So?" said Sienna impatiently.

Evie jumped up and looked at the magic map and then back at the treasure map. "Swan Lake is in the south… The academy is in the north… The stone circle is in the east… And the obelisk is in the west," she muttered. "That's it! They're at the four points of the compass!" She turned to the others, her eyes shining. "I think those things are the landmarks the riddle talks about. If you draw lines to join the four places up, the lines meet at a point in the middle – right here." She traced the lines in the air with her finger and pointed to a green mound in the centre of the magic map with a small rectangular monument on it. "I bet that's where we need to go."

"But the diamond can't be somewhere like that," said Lyra, peering at the small hill. "There's

almost nothing there –
definitely no maze."

Sienna gasped.
"Wait! I saw a
maze on the magic
map just now. I'm
sure I did." She
jumped up. "Yes!"
She pointed to a maze
of tall hedges to the north
west of the school. "Here."

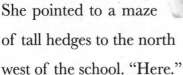

Ivy squealed. "There's a statue of Daybreak at
the centre!"

They swapped excited looks. In every one of
their adventures they'd had to find buttons that
had pictures of Daybreak, the first unicorn.

"Brilliant, Sienna!" said Lyra. "I bet that's
where the diamond is hidden."

Sienna glowed and tucked her corkscrew curls

behind her ears. "It's got to be, hasn't it? After all, the riddle says there's a maze." As she stared at the maze on the map, a thought struck her. What if she was the one who found the way through it first? If she held the diamond, she could make a wish. She didn't need to think about what her heart's desire was. If she wished that Sparkle had his magic and that he had bonded with her, then she'd be able to graduate with everyone else. She caught her breath. Could her idea actually work? "Let's go there now!" she burst out.

Evie looked doubtful. "I'm not sure. I think we should go where the landmarks meet."

Sienna shook her head. "The maze is obviously the right place."

"But—" Evie started to say.

Sienna was more desperate than ever to find the treasure and didn't let her finish. "No, Evie.

I know I'm right!" she said firmly.

Evie fell silent.

"Let's try!" said Lyra. She put her hand on the force field. "Magic map, please let us through," she begged. "We really need to go to the maze to find the diamond!" But the invisible wall stayed firm and solid. "The map's still not letting us use it," she said, disappointed.

"The maze is only about half a day's ride away," Sienna pointed out. "We could go tomorrow morning."

"No, we can't," said Ivy. "We have to practise our display for the graduation ceremony."

Sienna groaned. Each dorm had to do a display on graduation day for the parents when they would show off their unicorns' powers. She and Sparkle were part of Ruby dorm's display but because he hadn't found his magic yet there wasn't much for them to do apart from move

things into place for the others. She found it very boring. "Can't we skip practice?"

"No," said Lyra. "Our display has to be good."

"We could go to the maze in the afternoon, though," suggested Ivy. "We've got no lessons now, remember?"

They nodded. It was now so close to the end of term that lessons had stopped so they could prepare for graduation.

Lyra gathered up the map and they headed for the door, but Sienna hung back, taking one last look at the maze. Could she really get to the diamond before her friends?

Determination rushed through her. *You know what, I will!*

CHAPTER THREE

It was cold and wintery when the girls woke up the next morning. "Let's take our breakfast down to the stables and start practising our routine," said Lyra.

Sienna didn't move. "You lot go on ahead without me. Sparkle and I will turn into icicles if we have to stand around watching you all morning. I'm going to stay in bed a bit longer."

"Can't I stay in bed longer too?" moaned Ivy, who hated getting up.

"No!" said Lyra, plucking the duvet off her. "You need to get up!"

Evie came over to Sienna. "Please come and practise with us. It's more fun when we're all together."

Sienna shook her head. "It's boring watching you all do things when Sparkle and I can't join in. You go. I'll see you later."

She lay in bed, listening to their voices fading as they clattered down the stairs. Excitement started to fizz inside her as she remembered her idea from the night before. The others might be cross with her, but in the end they'd understand that she'd had to do it to graduate with them. And how amazing would it be to come back to the academy with the diamond and with Sparkle having found his magic?

Once she was sure the others would be busy practising their routine, she ran to the stables. There was no one else around; all the other students were busy practising for their displays.

Sienna and Sparkle

"Sparkle!" Sienna said excitedly, bursting into his stall. "Get ready – we're going on an adventure!"

"What, now?" Sparkle looked intrigued. "What kind of an adventure?"

"An adventure with just the two of us!" Sienna quickly explained her plan, leaving out the part where she used the diamond to wish for them both to graduate. "Let's go right away," she finished, heading out of his stall.

Sparkle hurried after her. "Sienna, wait! What about the others? We're supposed to be a team. Won't they be upset if you find the diamond without them?"

Sienna frowned. She wasn't used to Sparkle disagreeing with her. "Don't fuss, Sparkle. It'll be fine. They're really busy practising their graduation display. I'm just saving them the trouble of going to the maze." Sparkle still looked worried. "We have to go," she insisted. "If we find the diamond, we can—"

She broke off. What if he wasn't happy about her plan to make a wish with the diamond either?

"We can what?" he asked curiously.

"We can bring it back here and stop Dr Briar from getting it!" she said, continuing out into the stable yard. "Come on!"

"I'm really not sure about this," Sparkle said, following her.

"Well, I am," Sienna said impatiently. "I'm going to the maze, Sparkle. Are you coming with me or not?"

He gave in. "Of course I'll come."

Sienna felt a rush of triumph. "Awesome!"

She was about to climb on his back when she heard Ms Rosemary, the Care of Unicorns teacher calling her sharply. "Sienna!"

Heart sinking, she looked round.

From across the yard Ms Rosemary and Ms Nettles were striding towards her. "What are you doing?"

"I'm going for a ride," Sienna said.

"But look at Sparkle! You haven't groomed him. His mane and tail are full of straw; his coat has stains on. This is not good enough, Sienna." Ms Rosemary fixed her with a stern look. "Why are you going for a ride? Shouldn't you be with your dorm in the indoor arena working on your display?"

"They don't need me." Sienna was aware she sounded a bit sulky. "I can't do magic," she explained. "I can't do anything fun in the display, so I don't need to practise."

Ms Nettles raised her eyebrows. "The point is that you should be there to support your friends. It's not always about being the star; it's about being part of a team."

Sienna felt like pulling a face but she stopped herself. She did like being part of a team but only when there was a competition to win and everyone was cheering her on!

Ms Nettles studied her. "Sienna, you have the potential to be a wonderful guardian. You're strong and independent, brave and determined, and I don't want you to lose those qualities. However, you will not fulfil your potential unless you learn to be a team player."

Sienna sighed inwardly. Ms Nettles was so

annoying. *Blah, blah, blah.* She let her thoughts drift off to the maze. When she came back with the Unicorn's Diamond, Ms Nettles and Ms Rosemary would both have to admit she'd be a great guardian!

"Take Sparkle back into the stable and groom him properly," Ms Rosemary added crisply. "It's only one week to graduation.

You should spend every moment with Sparkle trying to bond and discover his magic."

Reluctantly, Sienna turned Sparkle round and headed back into the stables.

"Ms Nettles and Ms Rosemary are mean," said Sparkle, nuzzling her as she started to brush his mane.

"Yes," agreed Sienna.

"You'll be a brilliant guardian," Sparkle told her. "And you and I make a great team."

Sienna felt a flicker of guilt as she thought about her plan for the diamond.

"So what are we going to do now?" Sparkle asked. "Are we still going?"

Sienna hesitated. Although she felt cross with her teachers, she couldn't help hearing their words in her head and it was making her rethink. Maybe Sparkle was right. It wasn't a very team-like thing for them to go to the maze on their own. She knew how mad she'd be if one of the others decided to do that. And she might need their help. There was no reason why she couldn't go ahead of her friends once they

were in the maze and make sure she reached the diamond before anyone else. "We'll wait for the others," she said slowly.

Sparkle looked relieved. "Oh, good!"

After she had groomed him, they went outside. Sienna was just debating whether to join Ruby dorm in the arena – boring – or whether to go for a gallop in the meadows – much more fun – when Ivy came out of the arena and spotted her. "Sienna!" she called happily. "You've come to join in! Yay!"

Sienna forced a smile. She couldn't exactly go off now. "Yeah, I'm here," she said, riding Sparkle over to the arena where several other dorms were practising too.

It was a very dull morning watching the others. Misty made bubbles with her bubble magic and Sunshine exploded them. Flame shrank all the jumps dotted around as the others jumped

them before turning them back to their proper size. Sienna watched, half-heartedly calling out encouragement until she could join in with the crossnet skills and riding displays at the end.

"Well done, everyone," called Lyra as they got into a line and bowed.

"I'm worn out!" said Ivy, flopping on Flame's neck.

"Not so tired that you don't want to come out with the rest of us this afternoon, I hope," said Lyra.

Ivy smiled. "Definitely not." She lowered her voice to a whisper. "Imagine how exciting it will be if we actually find the you-know-what!"

"That might not be the only exciting thing that will happen." Lyra shot a meaningful look at Sienna and Sparkle.

Sienna's tummy lurched. Had Lyra guessed her plan? "What do you mean?" she said.

"Misty discovered her magic when we were out on an adventure. Maybe Sparkle will find his too," said Lyra.

Sienna breathed a sigh of relief.

"Oh, I hope Sparkle does discover his magic!" said Evie.

Sienna nodded quickly. "Me too!" If that happened, she wouldn't even need to make a wish on the diamond! But she decided she would still make sure she reached it first – just in case.

"This adventure is going to be fun!" Ivy said happily.

Sienna grinned. "Bring it on!"

CHAPTER FOUR

Ruby dorm gathered warm coats, gloves and everything else they needed and added it to the explorer's bag that Lyra always took with her when they went out. She kept all kinds of useful things in it like a compass, a penknife, a notebook, pens, torches and spare clothes. She also added a very large ball of string. "This might be useful when we're in the maze," she said. "If we tie the loose end to the entrance and then carry the ball with us, we'll be able to follow the string when we want to get out."

"We should also take some sky berries for the unicorns," said Ivy. "To revive their energy in case they have to do magic. And here are some biscuits for us!" She handed a bag over. "I asked the cook for some earlier."

"Great thinking," said Lyra. "Now remember, Dr Briar's unicorn, Solomon, has magic that lets him hear things that are happening elsewhere but *only* if they're happening outside. So, no mentioning the diamond when we set off just in case he's spying on us."

"Absolutely," said Evie, nodding seriously.

Ivy zipped her lips.

An uncomfortable thought wormed into Sienna's brain. She really hoped Solomon hadn't been listening in when she'd been talking to Sparkle earlier that morning about the maze!

Soon they were cantering away from school, the unicorns' hooves crunching on the frosty grass.

They rode out of the grounds and cantered along tracks that led through a wood of pine trees, then trekked across a flat valley before heading up a hill. Looking down from its summit they could see a patchwork of woods and fields laced with sparkling multicoloured rivers and streams. Sienna felt a rush of happiness. Unicorn Island was so beautiful! She couldn't wait to graduate

and become a guardian, protecting it and caring for it with Sparkle as her partner. *I will be a good guardian, whatever Ms Nettles and Ms Rosemary say*, she thought.

They rode on until they reached the maze, which was a sprawling mass of overgrown hedges, all far too high to see over.

"We're here!" Sienna said, riding Sparkle up to the entrance. "I guess we go in, find our way to the centre and hopefully that's where we'll find the—" She broke off, remembering Lyra's warning about Solomon's listening magic. "The you-know-what," she corrected herself.

Lyra frowned. "I'm pretty sure it won't be that easy. The pieces of the map were very hard to find. But let's get started." She took the ball of string out of her bag, carefully parted the branches of a big bush by the entrance and tied the loose end to its trunk. Then she handed the ball of string to Evie. "Can you ride at the back and carry this? Just let it

unravel as we go through the maze."

"OK," said Evie eagerly.

"Right, everyone, let's go!" Lyra jumped on to Misty's back, but before she could ride into the maze, Sienna clapped her heels to Sparkle's sides, making him leap forward. "I'll take the lead this time," she said.

Lyra looked slightly taken aback but nodded. "Sure. If you and Sparkle lead, it might help him find his magic."

"That would be brilliant!" said Ivy.

Guilt stabbed through Sienna as she thought about the real reason she wanted to be in the lead – to touch the diamond first and make a wish! *Only because I want to help Sparkle,* she told herself firmly. *I'm doing it for him.*

But are you really? a little voice in her head said.

She pushed it away and punched her hand into the air. "Follow me!"

They set off with Evie at the back, holding the ball of string and letting it gradually unravel. The maze had clearly not been looked after for years. The evergreen bushes arched overhead, forming a dark green tunnel. Bindweed and ivy trailed across the ground and thorny brambles caught at them as they passed. Birds fluttered in the branches and they saw the occasional flash of an animal moving through the undergrowth.

Sparkle halted at a fork in the path. "Which way now?" he asked. The two paths twisted away in opposite directions.

Sienna studied them carefully. "Let's go right." She wasn't sure but it seemed as good a guess as any!

The branches grew thicker on the right-hand path, forcing the unicorns to slow down as they waded through them.

"Is anyone else feeling spooked?" Ivy called out from behind.

"Me!" Evie's voice wobbled. "I think we're being followed. I'm sure I heard hooves just now."

"Lots of animals have hooves. It might be a three-antlered deer," said Sienna. "This place is like an animal hotel!" As if to prove her point, a storm racoon with a blue-and-grey ringed tail crossed the path, sprinting between Sparkle's hooves, before disappearing into another bush.

Everyone burst out laughing and they continued on, with Sienna making the choices at every fork and junction.

She was just beginning to think they would never get to the centre when they turned a corner and rode into a large square space with a moss-covered statue of Daybreak in the middle. "We're here!" cried Sienna.

She jumped off Sparkle and ran to the crumbling statue. Breathless with excitement, she looked around. *I have to find the diamond first*, she thought.

She hunted round the statue, but to her disappointment there was no obvious button or lever.

The others joined in, looking at every inch of the statue. Sienna even lay on the floor and looked at it from that way up.

"Nothing!" she said, scrambling up and brushing dirt from her jodhpurs. "Maybe it's in the bushes."

"No one would think that was a safe hiding place," Evie pointed out.

Lyra sighed. "I think we're in the wrong place, Sienna. There's nowhere a diamond could have stayed hidden for a hundred years."

Disappointment flooded through Sienna. She'd been sure this was where they needed to look and she hated being wrong. Everyone was probably thinking they should have listened to Evie.

Feeling irritable, she glanced at the ball of string Evie had dropped. A frown creased her forehead. The ball was much bigger than it should be given how far they'd ridden. She picked it up. The string felt loose, as though it wasn't attached to anything at the other end. Weird. Lyra had definitely tied it to the bush by the entrance. Sienna tugged on it gently and the end suddenly appeared. "It's come undone!" She swung round. "Evie, didn't you notice?"

Evie blushed. "Sorry! I was too busy looking around."

Sienna groaned. "Oh, Evie!"

Lyra hurried over. "I don't get it. I tied it really tightly." She picked up the end of the string and examined it. "It didn't come untied," she said grimly. "It's been cut!"

"But who would do that?" said Ivy.

"I'll give you one guess," said Lyra. "I bet Dr Briar and Solomon were listening in on us, then they used some kind of magic to come here and cut the string so we wouldn't be able to find our way out."

"But why?" asked Ivy.

Lyra shrugged. "Maybe Dr Briar thinks she

knows where the diamond is really hidden and she thought that if we were lost in here, we wouldn't be able to stop her from getting to it."

Sienna felt awful. It was her fault they'd come to the maze. She should have listened to Evie. Now it looked like Dr Briar was going to find the diamond before them. She felt like stamping in frustration. "We need to get out of here!" she said.

"I know," Lyra agreed, looking around. "But how?"

CHAPTER FIVE

"We could be wandering around in this maze for days," said Evie, going pale.

"We've only got a few biscuits!" said Ivy.

"Keep calm," said Lyra. "We'll find the way out if we work logically. Let's mark any paths that end up dead ends."

Misty whinnied excitedly. "Wait! I've got a better idea! Why don't we use my bubble magic, Lyra? My magic's much stronger now than it used to be. I think I can make a bubble that will float us all out."

Lyra hugged her. "Misty, you're a star."

Sienna and Sparkle

Everyone mounted their unicorns and formed a circle round Misty. She stamped her hooves, sending pink sparkles into the air. A gigantic shimmering bubble formed, surrounding everyone as it grew.

Misty stamped her hoof again and the bubble rose slowly up floating over the top of the maze. Looking down, the girls could see the twisting network of overgrown paths and intertwined

branches. The bubble came to rest on the grass near the maze's entrance. With a loud pop, it exploded.

Ivy and Evie burst out cheering and the other unicorns whinnied.

"Your magic's amazing, Misty!" cried Ivy.

"Just brilliant!" said Evie.

Misty's sides were heaving from the effort of doing so much magic.

"You're totally awesome." Lyra hugged Misty then fed her unicorn handfuls of sky berries from her bag.

Sienna watched jealously. If only Sparkle had found his magic and saved the day! *Nothing's gone right*, she thought grumpily.

Sparkle nudged her leg with his nose.

"What?" she said.

He looked pointedly at Misty. Sienna sighed. She knew what he wanted her to do but it was hard!

Still, Misty had been pretty amazing. She took a breath and forced a smile on her face. "You were great, Misty!" she called.

Misty looked round. "Thanks, Sienna!"

Lyra sent her a happy smile and to Sienna's surprise she felt her grumpiness fade slightly and be replaced by a warm glow. "I'm sorry I got us into a mess, guys," she said awkwardly.

"You didn't," said Ivy. "It wasn't your fault the string got cut."

"The diamond might have been hidden in this maze," Evie added.

"It's not your fault," said Lyra. "We work as a team, remember?"

Sienna fiddled with Sparkle's mane. "Yeah," she said uncomfortably. "We do."

After they'd arrived back at the stables and settled their unicorns, they headed to their dorm,

bumping into Sam. "Where have you lot been?" he said. "We've been trying to find you to see if you wanted a crossnet match."

"We've had more important things to do," said Lyra.

Sam looked interested. "You mean *treasure hunting*?" he said, lowering his voice. They nodded. He checked around to make sure no one else was there to overhear. "Did you find anything?"

Lyra explained where they'd been and what had happened in the maze.

Sam's face clouded with concern. "I bet you're right and Aunt Angelica cut the string. She really wants that diamond."

"But why?" Sienna burst out.

"She has to have the biggest collection of precious artefacts on the island. It's why she spends so much time supervising archaeological digs and exploring underground catacombs

and labyrinths. She likes being rich too though. Sometimes, when she's found something really valuable, she'll sell it to the highest bidder."

"But that means the diamond could end up in the hands of someone who wants to use it for evil," said Evie in alarm.

"We've really got to get hold of it before she does," said Lyra.

"The Unicorn's Diamond should only be used to wish for something that is good," said Ivy.

Her words made Sienna's tummy twist into knots. *But I do want something good. I want Sparkle to have his magic. It's what my friends want too. They'll be happy if I make that wish.*

Will they? The annoying little voice in her head spoke up again. *Or will they think it's cheating?*

"Are you coming to play crossnet?" Sam asked. "Or are you too chicken?"

Sienna pushed her troublesome thoughts away.

"Too chicken? In your dreams! Of course we'll play!"

Lyra and Ivy nodded but Evie didn't seem to have heard.

"Earth to Evie," said Sienna, waving a hand in front of her face. "Are you coming to play crossnet?"

"No," said Evie, shaking her head abruptly. "I need to go to the library!" Then she turned and hurried off.

The match was great fun. Especially, Sienna thought, because Ruby dorm won by two goals. When they finally got back to their room, they found Evie pacing around with an old dusty book open on her bed.

"I've got it!" she exclaimed. "I've worked it out!"

"What have you worked out?" said Lyra, confused.

"Where the diamond is!" They all gaped at

her. "It's in a maze but not the type we were thinking about," Evie rushed on. "It's in a maze that's under the ground!" She pointed at the book. It was open at a picture of a twisting network of tunnels. "Sam made me think of it. He mentioned  catacombs and labyrinths, so I went to the library and found this book and it says there's an underground labyrinth of tunnels at the centre of the island, hidden under that green mound I showed you on the magic map."

Lyra gasped. "So you were right all along. That's where we have to go?"

Evie's eyes shone. "I'm sure of it."

Ivy squealed and Lyra hugged Evie.

Sienna's mind raced. Although she hated to be wrong, what Evie was saying made perfect sense. She waited for Evie to say *I told you so* but she didn't.

"When should we go?" Evie asked excitedly.

"Right now!" said Lyra.

"Now?" Ivy echoed. "But it's almost dinner time and it's dark. Can't it wait until tomorrow? We could take a picnic with us then."

"We'd never get there and back in a day," said Evie. "It's miles away."

"How about we sneak out after dinner tonight when the teachers have gone to their rooms, fetch our unicorns, then ask the magic map to take us there?" said Lyra. "It didn't let us use it the other day but if we're right about the mound being the hiding place for the Unicorn's Diamond and it knows we're

trying to stop Dr Briar, then it might work."
She looked round at them all. "Let's try! We
can't let Dr Briar get there first. Agreed?"

"Agreed!" they all shouted.

CHAPTER SIX

When the girls went to give the unicorns their evening feeds, Sienna whispered their plan to Sparkle.

"Yay!" Sparkle said, stamping his hoof. "We're going hunting for—"

"Sssh!" Sienna said hastily. "Solomon might hear, remember!"

Sparkle nodded hard, his mouth pressed tightly shut, his eyes shining. He looked so cute that Sienna hugged him. She really was lucky to have him even if he hadn't found his magic yet.

And I'm lucky to have my friends, she thought as

they all trooped back to the school arm in arm. *None of them made me feel bad about going to the maze, not even Evie, and if we'd listened to her in the first place, we might have found the diamond by now.*

She was starting to feel more and more unsure about her plan to get to the diamond first. She didn't want to upset her friends. *But I really do want to graduate*, she thought, feeling torn.

Later, when the academy was quiet, the girls crept down the stairs. They ran across the frosty grass to get their unicorns, then rode them back to the hall.

The force field was humming softly as they approached it. The girls swapped looks. "Do you think it's going to let us use it?" Evie said.

Sienna took a deep breath. "Only one way to find out!" She rode towards the invisible barrier and the humming grew louder.

"Please," Sienna said softly. "Please let us past, magic map. I know I got it wrong before." The buzzing faded slightly and she felt encouraged. "Help us get to the mound at the centre of the island. We think the Unicorn's Diamond is there and we don't want Dr Briar to find it first."

The buzzing stopped completely. Sienna held her breath as she reached out a hand. The barrier had gone!

"We're through!" Turning, she saw the delight on her friends' faces and was relieved she'd abandoned her original plan of finding the diamond on her own. This was much more fun!

Everyone crowded round the map and the girls joined hands. With her free hand Sienna reached for the little hill at the centre of the island and touched its top. "Please take us to the labyrinth."

A wind sprang up, whirling Sienna's hair around her face. Sparkle's rainbow mane flew up too, and

the room began to spin faster and faster. The next moment, Sienna felt herself being whisked away.

The magic spun her and Sparkle around in the air and then they landed with a soft thud on springy turf. Sienna put out her hand just in time to catch a tiny model of Unicorn Academy. It had happened before when they'd used the map and she knew it would provide the fastest way of returning to school. Putting it safely in her coat pocket, she looked around.

They were standing next to a small grassy mound with a rectangular monument on top. It was engraved with names and had pictures of unicorns carved into the top.

"It's a monument to all the great unicorns who have lived on the island," said Evie, examining it in the moonlight.

Sienna looked round. A little way off was a huddle of trees. For a moment she thought she

saw a pale shape move in the shadows between the tree trunks, but a second later there was just darkness. She must have imagined it.

"Let's look for an entrance to the labyrinth," said Lyra, jumping off Misty.

They circled the monument, searching for a way in, running their hands over the stone and looking for secret buttons. Sienna dropped to her hands and knees and crawled round the base of the plinth, her fingers searching the stone until they discovered a gap. Her heart leapt as she probed it. "Lyra, can I borrow a torch?"

"Sure." Lyra rummaged for one in her explorer's bag.

Sienna shone the torch in the hole. The cavity was empty but the torch beam illuminated a stone circle at the back with a tiny picture of a unicorn crying a tear of joy. She gasped. "I've found a button with Daybreak on!"

"Press it!" urged Lyra.

Heart beating fast, Sienna pushed it. What would happen?

From deep inside the earth a rumbling started and the ground began to gently shake. Stone grated against stone and then slowly but surely the whole of the grassy mound sank into the ground, taking them all with it!

CHAPTER SEVEN

The mound descended into the ground like a grassy lift then stopped with a judder. Sienna blinked. It was so dark! She was still holding Lyra's torch and she swung it round.

The beam of light showed they were in a cave with dark tunnels twisting away in different directions.

Sienna felt a rush of excitement. "We're in the labyrinth!" She jumped on Sparkle's back and rode off the mound.

The others followed. Evie was last and as Sunshine's hooves touched the cave's floor the

ground began to shake and the grassy mound began to rise again. They watched as it fitted back into the hole in the ceiling, shutting them in the dark.

"How are we going to get out of here?" Ivy said with a quaver.

"We'll figure it out later!" Sienna answered, too excited to worry about that yet. "Which way to find the diamond?"

She shone the torch around. Each tunnel had pictures carved above its entrance. "Let's try this

one," she said, pointing at the widest tunnel.

The others nodded. "OK," said Lyra. "You can lead."

Sienna smiled at her. She knew Lyra loved to be the leader, but she was holding back because she wanted Sparkle to find his magic. "Thanks."

"Wait, Sienna. What about going down this tunnel?" said Sparkle. "The floor is smoother, like someone has walked down it before. Maybe it was Ms Evergreen when she hid the diamond?"

Sienna frowned. She didn't agree. "But it twists back on itself." She shone the torch into his tunnel to show how it curved. "It could end up back here."

"But—"

"I'm sure it's this way," said Sienna impatiently.

Sparkle snorted unhappily but to Sienna's relief he walked into the tunnel she'd chosen. The others rode after her with Lyra bringing up the rear. The

tunnel twisted and turned until it reached a dead end. "Oh," Sienna said in disappointment.

"We'd better turn round," said Lyra.

They struggled to turn in the tight space and Lyra ended up leading them back to the main cave.

"I wish you'd listen to me," Sparkle said crossly to Sienna.

She frowned in surprise. He was hardly ever grumpy with her. "What's the matter with you?" she asked.

"Nothing," he muttered.

When they were back in the first cave, Ivy said, "Let's look at the carvings above each tunnel. Maybe one of them is a clue."

"Spread out, everyone, and see what you can find," Sienna instructed.

They all did as she said and hunted around.

"Here!" said Ivy at last. "On the wall above this

tunnel, there's a carving of a bird rising from a fire. That's what phoenixes do."

"Maybe it's something to do with the *Phoenix's Claw* on the map," said Lyra, joining her on Misty.

Evie gasped. "Hang on! Do you think all those things on the map are clues to help us find our way through the labyrinth? *The Northernmost Door… The Phoenix's Claw… The Salamander's Stare… The Dragon's Lair…*"

Sienna whooped. "I bet you're right! Come on, everyone!"

She rode Sparkle down the tunnel that had the phoenix above it – it was the tunnel Sparkle had originally suggested. The others clattered after her.

But to Sienna's intense disappointment, the new tunnel also ended in a brick wall.

"Let's not give up yet," said Lyra, jumping off Misty and starting to hunt around. "There may be something here we just haven't seen yet… Yes!"

She pointed to a round indentation in the wall. "A button!"

Sienna punched the air. "Yay! Press it!"

Lyra pressed the button that had a carving of Daybreak on it. There was a loud grating sound and the wall slid open to reveal a hidden chamber, the walls lit by a soft blue fluorescent glow that was coming from little blue flowers growing on the walls.

Wow!" breathed Sienna. "Let's go in."

"But it might not be safe," said Sparkle, not moving.

Sienna rolled her eyes. "Don't be silly. This has to be the way."

Sparkle stepped cautiously inside and the others followed.

Ivy was the last to enter and as she and Flame crossed the threshold there was a loud rumbling sound.

"What's that?" said Evie warily.

They all gasped as the wall closed behind them with a crash.

"We're trapped!" said Ivy in alarm.

"We can't be. There's bound to be a way out," said Sienna. "Look, there's another tunnel over there."

She started to ride towards it, but the walls began to shake and stones rained down on them from the roof.

Ivy shrieked as one hit her. "Ow!"

The noise grew louder and suddenly Sienna realised that the walls and roof had started to move. A wave of

fear overwhelmed her. "The cave's closing in!" she yelled. "We're going to be crushed!"

"Gallop!" shouted Lyra, pointing at the tunnel straight ahead.

Sparkle leapt after Misty, his hooves clattering and skittering as they galloped across the stone-strewn floor. Sienna lay over his neck, making herself as flat as she could as the roof pressed closer. Sparkle raced into the escape tunnel, with Ivy right behind them. Evie and Sunshine were the last. Looking round, Sienna gasped. The walls had reached them, touching Sunshine's sides. They weren't going to make it!

Evie shrieked. "Help! We're going to be crushed!"

CHAPTER EIGHT

Sunshine stopped galloping and reared up, stamping her hooves down hard on the ground. Magical sparks crackled around her, shooting into the air, followed by a deafening bang. The walls about to crush her and Evie exploded into dust. Evie screamed and covered her head as she was pelted by flying rock. Luckily Sunshine's explosion had been so powerful that the pieces were very small.

"Sunshine, you saved my life!" Evie said, hugging her as they staggered out of the dusty chamber. "You're the best unicorn ever!"

Lyra jumped down and scrambled over the rocks to feed Sunshine handfuls of sky berries to get her strength back.

"What happened?" asked Ivy, waving her hands around at the remains of the cave. "Why did the walls move?"

Lyra looked grim. "The cave's been booby-trapped."

"By Dr Briar?" asked Sienna in horror.

"I don't think so," said Lyra. "There'd be no point in her setting the traps if she'd already been here and found the diamond. I think they were set by Ms Evergreen when she hid the Unicorn's Diamond to try to stop anyone finding it."

"Well, her traps won't stop us!" declared Sienna.

"Agreed," said Ivy firmly.

"But we'd better be careful. There could be more traps," Evie added.

Sienna nodded and led the way along the

tunnel. After a while it began to narrow and slope downhill until it came to a crossroads. Sienna shone her torch around and spotted a carving of a door above one of the tunnels. It had a compass face above it, the arrow facing north. "*The Northernmost Door!*" she breathed.

"Looks like we have to go this way," said Lyra, setting off. She stopped herself. "Sorry, Sienna, you go."

"It's OK," said Sienna. She'd stopped thinking about getting to the diamond first. All she wanted was for them to find it and get out safely!

They rode slowly on, the unicorns placing their hooves with care. Sienna heard a dull roar in the distance. *Was it a waterfall?* The roar got louder and louder and eventually they pulled up on the edge of a vast river that roared and foamed.

"How do we get across that?" Ivy said.

"There," said Sienna, nodding at a series of

flat stepping stones that started at the bank and crossed the river in a wonky line.

Evie's face creased with worry. "They look very wobbly."

"Sparkle and I will go first," said Sienna. "Don't worry."

"But, Sienna, it really doesn't look safe," Sparkle protested.

"It'll be fine," Sienna told him.

Sienna and Sparkle

Sparkle took a tentative step forward, putting a hoof on the first stepping stone, but as he transferred his weight the stone rocked violently and disappeared into the frothing water. Sparkle leapt back in the nick of time, but his back hooves slipped, and for one horrible moment Sienna thought they were going to slide into the rushing river.

"Sparkle!" she shrieked.

Sienna's unicorn managed to regain his footing but she could feel him shaking with the shock.

"That was close," said Lyra, wide-eyed.

"The stepping stones must be booby-trapped too," said Misty. "Why don't I use my bubble magic to float us across?

"Go for it, Misty," said Lyra, stroking her.

Misty stamped her hoof and a silvery bubble rose around everyone. It picked them up and carried them safely over the rushing water. It

came to rest on the other side before popping and releasing them. They all breathed a collective sigh of relief.

"Well done, Misty!" said Evie.

"That was brilliant!" said Ivy.

Sienna joined in too. "Your magic's amazing!"

Misty looked pleased. "Thank you!"

Sienna felt the same warm glow that she'd felt when she'd complimented her after they'd escaped from the outdoor maze. "Misty did really well, didn't she?" she whispered to Sparkle as Lyra fed her some sky berries.

"Mmm," Sparkle muttered. His head was low and he didn't look at her. Sienna frowned. He was being very weird. She was about to ask him what the matter was when Lyra called out, "Misty's recovered now. Let's go on."

They set off down a tunnel leading away from the river. A short while later it ended in another

dead end. There were some carvings on the stone wall in front of them. They all crowded round.

Lyra's torch beam picked out a picture of a spotted lizard facing sideways. Its eye was large and staring.

"That's a salamander," said Ivy, who knew a lot about animals.

"And the clue was *The Salamander's Stare*," said Lyra.

"Look at its eye!" Evie exclaimed. They all looked more closely. The salamander's eye wasn't actually an eye at all; it was button that had a picture of Daybreak on it.

Evie pushed the button, and slowly the wall began to rise before disappearing into the tunnel's roof.

"Whoa!" Sienna's eyes grew wide as she took in the cavern now open in front of them. Its roof arched high overhead. Its walls were made of

rose quartz and there were unicorn statues inside it carved from the same sparkly pink rock, some playing, others leaping and galloping.

"What a beautiful place," Ivy breathed, riding Flame inside.

But then Sienna heard the sudden grinding of stone. "What's that?"

To her horror a huge boulder detached from the far wall of the cavern and started rolling towards them like a giant bowling ball. "It's another trap!" she yelled.

CHAPTER NINE

Sienna stared, terrified, as the boulder sped towards them, ploughing through the beautiful statues and smashing them to smithereens. It was so huge there was no way of avoiding it.

"We're going to be squished!" shouted Ivy, turning pale.

"Don't worry – I've got this, Ivy!" Flame cried.

He stamped his hooves on the ground, making orange sparks fly up. The cavern was suddenly flooded with the scent of magic and the sparks hit the boulder. A cracking sound echoed around and the boulder shrank to the size of a marble.

It carried on rolling but Flame stopped it with a hoof.

Ivy squealed and hugged him. "You saved us!"

Sienna breathed out shakily. "That was really close. Well done, Flame. Let's get out of here right now." She didn't want to spend another moment in the booby-trapped cavern.

The unicorns picked their way round the chunks of statue that now littered the ground. Evie, Ivy and Lyra were talking about the boulder, but Sienna didn't join in. She couldn't ignore the fact that Sparkle didn't seem his normal self. "Are you all right, Sparkle? You seem quiet."

Sparkle sighed heavily. "I feel useless, Sienna," he confessed. "Sunshine used her exploding magic to stop us from being crushed by the moving walls. Misty used bubble magic to help us over the river and Flame used his shrinking magic to save us from the boulder. What have I done to help? Nothing."

"Oh, Sparkle! Don't be like that." Sienna stroked his neck. "Just because they have their magic doesn't make them better than you."

He turned his head to look at her. "You wouldn't rather have a different unicorn?"

"Of course not!" she said in surprise. "Why would you even think that?"

He snorted awkwardly. "It's just you never seem to listen to me and—"

He was interrupted by Lyra who had reached a fork in the path. "There's a carving of a dragon here." She pointed to a dragon above the left-hand fork. "I guess we go this way."

"I hope it's not a real dragon," said Evie.

"Who knows in this place!" said Ivy with a shiver.

"Do you and Sparkle want to go first, Sienna?" Lyra asked.

"Is that OK with you, Sparkle?" said Sienna.

She had stopped thinking about getting to the diamond first to get a wish, but the labyrinth was so dangerous she was happy to go first and protect her friends – as long as Sparkle agreed.

He nodded. "We'll lead the way!"

He set off down the tunnel. It ended in a wall with an opening in it. Sitting in it was a three-headed stone dragon. As Sienna rode closer to investigate, its three gaping mouths puffed out tiny flames. Sienna took a breath. The dragon didn't look that bad in comparison to the other dangers they'd faced…

Ping! Ping! Ping! A deadly silver arrow shot out from each of the dragon's three mouths and raced towards her head. She shrieked and ducked, only narrowly avoiding being hit. "Go back!" she yelled to Sparkle but before he could turn, three more arrows came firing out.

There was no time to escape – only to fight! Holding her torch as if it was a rounders bat, Sienna swatted the first arrow away. She heard gasps from her friends behind her as she struck the second and the third arrow and sent them flying. With the third arrow dispatched, Sienna raised her arms in victory. "Take that, arrows!"

"Duck!" shrieked Lyra as the dragon fired another round. These ones were even bigger and faster than those before!

WHAM! WHAM! WHAM! Sienna batted them away one after the other, but she was beginning to tire. Her arms were aching. Sparkle must

have sensed her fatigue because he nickered his support. "Keep going. You can do this!"

There was an ominous pause and then suddenly a lone arrow shot out. It was much bigger than the other arrows and it flamed with fire.

"Get it, Sienna!" Sparkle whinnied.

With one last effort Sienna belted it away. It hit the wall and dissolved into sparks.

The others whooped and cheered. The flames puffing out of the dragon's mouths flickered and died.

Sparkled twisted his head to nuzzle her leg. "That was awesome," he said. "You were amazing."

"I'm so glad that was you and not me, Sienna!" said Evie in relief, riding Sunshine over to her.

"Me too. None of the rest of us could have hit all those arrows like that," added Lyra.

Ivy joined in, congratulating Sienna and telling her how brilliant she was, but Sienna could barely take it in. She felt very shaky. If she hadn't managed to bat those arrows away, one of her friends or their unicorns might have been badly hurt. She was so glad they were all safe!

Suddenly she realised just how much they all meant to her. Ruby dorm and their unicorns were a team and she was part of it. It didn't matter whether she was scoring the winning goal or batting deadly

arrows away or telling her friends how great they were – the important thing was being there for them, just like they were there for her.

A loud rattle startled her out of her thoughts. The three-headed dragon had swivelled round and gold flames were erupting from its mouths. They hit the wall at the back of the opening and the stones and dragon vanished. All that was left was an entrance to another vast cavern.

Sienna gulped. What was waiting for them this time? Cautiously she walked forward and looked inside.

"Oh, wow!"

CHAPTER TEN

The cavern was huge, the biggest and most beautiful yet. Its walls were studded with glittering gems, and in the centre was a snow-white marble pillar. On top of this was an enormous diamond. Clearer than crystal, the diamond sparkled with hope and promise.

Almost in a trance, Sienna slid from Sparkle's back and walked forward. Beside the diamond was a silver square with words engraved on it.

To you who triumphed and found this stone,
My traps stopped one person from acting alone.
If you seek the diamond for selfish ends,

Stop — use its power for good, my friends.

Sienna lifted the diamond up, feeling the tingle of its power passing over her skin. Her thoughts raced as she made up her mind…

"STOP!" a hard voice rang out.

"Sienna!" Evie squeaked.

Sienna swung round and saw that Dr Briar had crept up on the group. Riding Solomon, a tall proud-looking unicorn, she was armed with a long ceremonial sword. Dr Briar had her arm round Evie's neck and was touching the tip of the sword to Evie's throat. Her eyes glittered with menace.

Sienna gasped. "Dr Briar! How did you get here?"

Dr Briar's lips curved in a cruel smile. "Solomon and I have been using cloaking magic to follow you through the labyrinth. I have to say it was very useful to have you to lead us safely through

the traps. You did very well to reach the diamond. However, if you value your friend's life, then you will bring it to me."

"We'll see about that!" Flame whinnied, stamping his hooves. There was a flash of light and Dr Briar's sword shrank to the size of a pin. She gave a shout of surprise.

"Guess you're not going to have it, after all," said Sienna, waving it at her. "Finders keepers!"

"Give it to me!" Dr Briar screeched, jumping off Solomon and striding towards her.

"No way!" said Sienna.

Dr Briar screamed and leapt at her, grappling with her for the diamond.

Sienna staggered, lost her grip and the glittering gem flew into the air.

Dr Briar jumped, trying to catch the diamond as it fell.

"Oh no you don't!" Sienna yelled, leaping to catch the diamond too. Her fingers closed round it. "Yes!"

But, just as she landed, Dr Briar pulled a brooch from her jacket and drove the pin into Sienna's leg.

Sienna fell to the ground in pain. The diamond landed on the floor and rolled away.

With a furious whinny Sparkle charged at Dr Briar, who was scrabbling after the diamond. "No one hurts Sienna!" His eyes blazed and he looked completely furious. He butted Dr Briar hard with his head and she fell backwards.

Misty stamped a hoof and a bubble instantly formed around Dr Briar. She hammered her hands against its sides but the bubble stayed firm.

Sienna whooped. "Go, Misty!"

94

"And Sunshine!" cried Evie as Sunshine exploded a boulder at Solomon's feet, sending the taller unicorn skittering backwards. Sunshine exploded another boulder and then another. Solomon turned and was about to gallop away into the labyrinth when Misty captured him in a bubble too.

Sparkle had reached Sienna. "Sienna! Are you OK? How's your leg?"

"It's fine," Sienna said, not wanting to make a fuss.

"No, it's not!" he insisted. "Let me see." He nudged her hand away and his eyes widened in alarm. "You're hurt!" He stamped his hoof on the ground in dismay. Sienna gasped as rainbow sparkles flew up from the floor. They rained down gently on her leg and she watched in disbelief as the edges of the wound suddenly knitted together and the pain faded to tingles and then to nothing.

"Sparkle, w-was that you?" she stammered, getting to her feet.

"I ... I think I've found my magic," he breathed.

"Sparkle's got healing magic!" Lyra cried happily.

Sienna threw her arms round Sparkle's neck. "I can't believe it. I'm so happy for you!"

"For us!" Sparkle said, his eyes shining. "And, look, we've bonded." He nuzzled Sienna's hair. One dark corkscrew curl was now a rainbow of colour.

Sienna squealed with joy and hugged Sparkle again while her friends whooped and their unicorns stamped their hooves.

"Where's the diamond?" said Lyra suddenly.

She started to hunt for it. Ivy and Evie joined in, but Sienna didn't care about the diamond any more. She wanted to talk to Sparkle. She stroked his face. "I'm sorry it's taken this long to find your magic. Ms Nettles was right. It was my fault. I thought I was good at teamwork because I'm good at winning but that's not what it's about. Being in a team means supporting your teammates, listening and being happy when good stuff happens to them. From now on I'll remember that – with you and the others. Being in a team is great!" She kissed him. "Particularly when it's a team with your best friend."

Sparkle nuzzled her. "Am I your best friend?"

Sienna glanced at Lyra, Evie and Ivy. They were all brilliant – she knew she'd be friends with them for the rest of her life – but they weren't Sparkle. The bond she had with him was extra-special. "You are," she said softly.

He sighed happily. "And you're mine too. It's not your fault we didn't find my magic. This adventure has made me realise I'm not good at speaking up. I need to get better at saying what I think and feel. I shouldn't always just agree with you, particularly when we're in a dangerous situation."

"So we're both going to change," said Sienna.

"Yes, but you're still allowed to like winning and I'm still allowed to agree with you most of the time!"

"Deal!" said Sienna, laughing and kissing his forehead.

"Sienna," Lyra called anxiously, "we can't find the diamond! It's vanished!"

Sienna bit her lip. "I might have had something to do with that."

They all stared at her.

"What did you do?" asked Evie, astonished.

She grinned. "When I held it for those few seconds I wished for my heart's desire." As soon as she had felt the diamond's power she had known what she should wish for. No matter how desperate she was for Sparkle to find his magic and for them to be able to graduate with their friends, the island would always come first. She had to protect it. "I wished for the diamond to be somewhere safe, where no one could ever use it to harm Unicorn Island."

The others gasped and then rushed over to hug her.

"That was genius, Sienna!" said Lyra.

"I'd never have thought of that," said Ivy.

"So where do you think it went?" asked Evie.

Sienna shrugged. "No idea. But who cares, so long as it's safe."

"Totally," said Lyra. "Now we should get back and tell Ms Nettles what Dr Briar's been up to.

It's been an amazing adventure even if we're not going back with the diamond. Just solving the clues and finding it has been enough."

Sienna smiled round at her friends. Lyra was right. They'd had so much fun – who cared if they didn't have the treasure in their hands?

Sienna searched in her pockets for the model of the academy. She climbed back on Sparkle, then holding the model in her hand she spoke clearly, "Please take us back to the academy."

A wind swirled about her, lifting everyone off the ground and whisking them away.

CHAPTER
ELEVEN

"It's the girls!"

"They're back!"

Sienna opened her eyes and saw that they were back in the hall beside the magic map. Sam, the rest of the boys from Topaz and their unicorns were standing alongside Ms Nettles who was dressed in a long nightie, pink fluffy dressing gown and unicorn slippers.

"We've been so worried! We went into your room to see if you wanted a midnight feast and found you gone," said Sam. "I guessed you must have used the map to sneak out, but when you

didn't come back I thought Aunt Angelica might have trapped you so I told Ms Nettles."

"Whatever happened?" said Ms Nettles. "Sam's been telling me all sorts of things – treasure maps … the Unicorn's Diamond…"

Ruby dorm explained everything. Ms Nettles listened, her eyebrows occasionally arching with astonishment.

"Well," she said when they had finished, "I wish that you'd thought to show me the map first. Ms Evergreen was famous for her dangerous traps that could only be outwitted by teamwork. If I'd have known about it, I would never have let you go into the labyrinth."

Sienna was very glad they hadn't told Ms Nettles about the map. Imagine missing out on such an awesome adventure! Glancing at her friends she was certain they were all thinking the same thing.

Ms Nettles continued. "But, since you didn't, I'm relieved you didn't use the diamond for your own gain but used the magic to put it somewhere safer. A place where no one can use it for evil purposes." She smiled at Sienna. "And, Sienna, well done for helping Sparkle find his magic and bonding! It may have taken a while but you have no doubt learnt valuable lessons along the way. I have every faith that you will both make excellent guardians.

As for Dr Briar, she will be dealt with appropriately when we track her down."

"You don't need to track her down," said Sienna. "She's still in the centre of the labyrinth in a giant bubble, thanks to Misty. The map will be able to take you to her."

"And don't forget Solomon," added Ivy. "He's in a bubble too."

"They will be punished," said Ms Nettles sombrely.

Sienna nodded, but she didn't care what happened to Dr Briar as long as she couldn't ever get her hands on the diamond!

Ms Nettles smiled warmly. "I imagine you must all be very hungry after your adventures. Take your unicorns back to the stables and make sure they get a large helping of sky berries, then hurry back to the dining hall. I think it's time for that midnight feast!"

A week later, Sienna, Sparkle and all her friends from both Ruby and Topaz dorms gathered in the hall again, this time for the graduation ceremony. Their unicorns had been brushed until their coats shone, their manes and tails were plaited, and their hooves sparkled with brightly coloured polish.

The display had gone really well. Watched by their parents, the unicorns had showed off their magic. Sparkle's healing magic had been trickier to demonstrate than everyone else's magic, but he'd revived an almost dead bouquet of flowers. However, Sienna had found she didn't mind not being the centre of attention for once and she'd cheered loudly as her friends showed off their magic, and her chance to shine had come at the end when they concluded their display with a demonstration

of their crossnet skills. Evie held the goal up while Ivy passed the ball to Lyra, who passed it to Sienna, who then scored an awesome goal at a flat-out gallop. The audience applauded as, leaning down, Sienna effortlessly scooped the ball back up with her stick, threw it backwards over her shoulder and scored again. The audience went wild and Sienna galloped round grinning.

After the graduation ceremony, there was a banquet in the hall before everyone drifted outside for the traditional firework display. Sienna and her friends gathered together, swapping addresses with the boys and promising to meet up soon.

As the fireworks started with a hiss and a bang, lighting up the starry sky, Sienna put an arm round Sparkle's neck. "We did it! We graduated together after all."

"We've still got tons to learn," said Sparkle. "This is just the start of our adventures."

Sienna agreed. "I'm going to miss this place and all our friends, but I can't think of anyone I'd rather share the journey with."

Sparkle pressed his cheek to her face. "Me neither."

They stood for a moment then Sparkle suddenly pulled away. "Sienna, what's that star?" He nodded to a bright star high up in the sky. It was shaped like a teardrop and twinkling like a diamond. "I've never seen it before."

Sienna drew in a breath as she considered it. "Could it be the Unicorn's Diamond?"

"You did wish for it to be put somewhere safe where no-one would be able to use it to harm the island," said Sparkle in delight.

Sienna hugged Sparkle, happiness rushing

through her as the fireworks exploded around them and the bright new star cast its sparkling light over the beautiful island.